Caught In The Act

AMY LAURENS

OTHER WORKS

Find other works by the author at www.amylaurens.com

Caught In The Act

INKLET #93

AMY LAURENS

Inkprint
PRESS

www.inkprintpress.com

Print ISBN: 978-1-922434-34-0
eBook ISBN: 9798201841331

www.inkprintpress.com

National Library of Australia Cataloguing-in-Publication Data
Laurens, Amy 1985 –
Caught In The Act
76 p.
ISBN: 978-1-922434-34-0
Inkprint Press, Canberra, Australia
1. Fiction—Science Fiction—Crime & Mystery 2. Fiction—Short Stories

First Print Edition: November 2022
Cover photo © Outsiderzone via Deposit Photos
Cover design © Inkprint Press
Interior art © Amy Laurens

CAUGHT IN THE ACT

*** * BEGIN RECORDING, SOUND BOOTH 108 061248 154801 * ***

[A male voice, energetic and full of verve, begins.]

Okay. Here we go. Boy are you gonna love the evidence I have to show you. Just letting you know, I'll need to translate the resonance recordings for you live, I haven't done a formal translation of them yet.

I'll try to keep my asides brief.

So, to give you some context before we begin, the parties:

In the following tapes, we will encounter Kate, mastermind and notably good citizen, who'd never committed anything more outrageous than parking for three hours in a two-hour parking zone before this and insists on wearing vanilla perfume everywhere. At five four with an average build, olive skin and brown hair, there's nothing terribly remarkable about her appearance—apart from that look of fierce determination in her eyes, and a resemblance to someone we'll meet later on.

Then there's Phil, dry-witted and unflinching gaze, who never actually committed crimes himself, because that would be both foolhardy and against his personal moral code—but who's served as a distraction more times than he cared to admit to his wife—or his interviewer. (Cops found the records though, of course.) Phil's five eleven, average build, fair skin, red hair cropped in a neat, professional contour.

And there's Gus, six two, broad build, dark olive skin, black hair, who lived out ninety percent of his life as a gentle giant, a popular Santa Claus impersonator, a favourite of everyone everywhere in his life—and whose secret, lifelong passion for weaponry made him easily the most dangerous person in any room.

Really, with his job, someone should've seen that one coming at least.

Okay. First piece of evidence. It's a resonance recording. You mind if I put my earbuds in for this one? You wouldn't understand it if you could hear it anyway, and I get a lot more detail with the sound up close.

Thanks.

Right.

Item 1: State Resonance Recording 163-501B 26/19

The room is hot. Sweat keeps dripping down the back of Kate's neck until, fed up, she bundles her dark hair up into the hair band she's had on her wrist.

See visual footage from building's reception security camera, 21:56 on the night in question to confirm.

Sitting opposite her at the cheap wooden table is Gus. He's also dealing with dripping sweat. It isn't any place as kosher as his neck.

Only Phil, sardonic smile on his lips as though in his head he's mocking Kate (yes, al*right*, I can't read that in the resonances, but honestly, it's just his natural expression, it's hardly a far-fetched guess—okay *fine, yes, sorry*, I'll stick to what I can pull from the resonance recording)—only Phil seems immune from the heat.

(And I can tell *that* from the resonances, *thanks*, because he isn't shifting around, swiping and itching at himself.)

(Look, I'll strike these asides from the official transcript later, okay? Make it all pretty for your bosses. Do you want me to translate the resonance recording for you or not?)

Ahem.

One wonders why they don't turn the air-conditioning on.

Perhaps they're afraid of being discovered; the little room they've chosen to plot their crimes in is hardly inconspicuous: an empty office meeting room, after hours at Gus's place of employ, i.e. the local hardware wholesaler.

I went to Hard!Ware! several weeks after the event, after I realised the connection. It stank of metal and cleaning polish, and the peculiar, tinny taste of the capsules I can only really describe as *blue*.

Gunmetal blue, perhaps.

There *was* an air conditioner in the room. It did make an awful, dying-cat rattle when I turned it on. Like it had been inhaling smoke all these years and its internals were giving out.

Fear of discovery would also explain why the resonance indicates a lack of lighting in the room at the time.

(*Yes*, I can tell that, the place still uses old-style fluorescent lights and they put a buzz in the recording.)

…Look, you seem like you're in a hurry, do you want a full transcription for this, or just the highlights? You get the picture, there are people in a meeting room, hot as hell, they're trynna be secretive, la la.

Okay cool, I'm just going to give you the dialogue.

It cuts in partway through, we're pulling this from UTC's general surveillance satellite.

Why?! Well it's not like we *knew* this was gonna happen and were actively surveilling. Shesh. You're lucky we got this at all, mate.

Right, where was I up to… Right, okay, this is the dialogue.

Kate: …ready to go?

Gus: Yep. Ready and steady.

Phil: Right as rain, too?

Kate: Shut up, Phil. Save your attitude for the guards.

Phil: Yes'm.

Kate: Don't give me that crap.

Gus: Phil, leave her alone. You wanna try to pull this without her?

(There's silence for a bit, pretty sure it's Kate who's pacing back and forth.)

Kate: Okay, let's just go over the entrance strategy one more time, okay? Phil?

Phil: (he's in serious mode now) 3pm. I'm outside the clinic. I "strike up a conversation" with the guard.

Kate: I walk in, Jennifer Lovegood here for her capsule appointment. Gus?

Gus: (he grunts) I'm in the car, corner of Fourth and Main out back. Laundry truck arrives, I hit it with the atomiser, nick a uniform, get out of there.

Kate: Perfect. Okay. Appointment. They take me to the vault. I tag the capsule we're gonna hit.

Gus: I still don't see why we can't take more than one. There's three of us here running this, oughta be three capsules going out.

Kate: (witheringly) You *trying* to get caught?

(Course, he doesn't realise yet that they all will be anyway, heh.)

Phil: Look, man, you gotta trust Kate or what else've you got? You'n me couldn't pull this off alone and you know it. Where are you gonna get an atomiser from at this late notice?

Gus grunts.

There's a big inhale-exhale thing, I think it's Kate again.

Kate: I go in. I tag the vault. I go out back. I meet Gus on the outside with the atomiser and a uniform he's snitched from the laundry truck. Phil does his thing with the guard—you got your look-at-mes?

(I presume Phil nods, but right at this moment Gus is shifting his sweat around again so it's a little hard to read over the interference.)

Kate: Great. I go back in, this time in uniform. Phil follows, does his thing with the receptionist. I sneak back to the vault. Atomiser does its thing. I head out back where Gus and Phil are waiting in the car. Bam. Case closed.

Phil: Unless you buzz for help.

Kate: Unless I buzz for help. In which case…

Gus: I get to bring out my toys. (The most enthusiastic we've heard him yet.)

Kate: Right. I hope you don't have to, but if you do, you're gonna have to put in everything you've got. They catch up, we're going to Orbit.

(There's a bit of a pause, they're all unnaturally still. Not sure if they heard something that spooked 'em, or if they're all just contemplating the idea of ending up in orbit on Deto, locked away for life.)

Gus: I dunno. You really think we're gonna pull it off?

Kate: No, that's why I'm risking my life with a pair of dumbasses to rob the biggest clinic in the country. Idiot. Look, we're good. I'm not gonna say 'what could go wrong', because that's just dumb, but seriously. We're ready. We're good. We can do this.

Gus shrugs.

Phil: …Kate? You… sure you're telling us everything?

(I can only imagine Kate shooting him a scathing, withering look right about now. It tracks. Trust me.)

Phil: Yeah. Yeah okay.

That's all we've got of their conversation—satellite moved out of range after that. But you get the gist. Here, this next one's more interesting, the video footage from the clinic.

You're, ah, technically not supposed to see this one until I've formally transcribed it for the court, though. So, uh, I'm gonna transcribe it now, okay?

Just budge up over there, and I can close the sound screen properly, and that way you're not in here and if you happen to be watching a transcribe tech doing their job, well, what of it, right?

Right. Thanks. Much obliged.

Item 2: Security Footage from Lifetime Clinic, 256 Aeon Drive, Walang Kamatayan, AC 163-501B 27/19

Transcriber's note: This transcription is based on footage pieced together from the cameras collectively feeding Walang Kamatayan's Lifetime Clinic.

It's the reception of the Walang Kamatayan Lifetime Clinic, the largest clinic in AC. And it looks it: the reception foyer isn't huge for a room, but it's clearly a room where they expect a lot of people to be waiting—perhaps the size of an average living room, if one's average living room had black marble flooring and sleek, chromed futuristic chairs.

There are plants dotted around the room, large ferns in expensive ceramic pots in the corners (the pots all green and blue, of course, to match the Lifetime brand) and pink and white orchids in black pots everywhere else, the pots' black lacquer contrasting texturally with the sleek, mirror-black reception desk.

Like Hard!Ware!, I visited Lifetime not long after this recording was taken. Then, it smelled of burnt plastic and ash, but on the day of this recording we can presume that it was as freshly orchid-scented as every other Lifetime clinic, with that blue, tinny taste in the back of your throat caused by the high concentration of capsules moving in and around the clinic.

On the recording, we can see that the large waiting room is empty. The air conditioning is obviously on—the larger plants bob and wave a little in the breeze it generates and, more to the point, the receptionist—fair skin-ned, yellow—sorry, *golden*—haired, approximately five ten, slim build—sits quietly behind the reception desk with nary a stray hair nor the sheen of sweat. She's cool, she's calm, she's refreshed, she's ageless—in short, she's everything Lifetime claims to provide.

The front door chimes, a modest, ethereal sound, and our protagonist Kate walks in.

Better, she strides in like she owns the place, black three-inch stilettos tap-tap-tapping on the marble.

(Have to give it to her, the woman has acting *skillz*.)

She's got a full face of makeup on and she's giving the receptionist a run for her money in terms of that dewy, ageless face look.

The receptionist glances up—and if you watch the recording very carefully, it's possible to catch the minute flash of disgust that crosses her face, as though the sour taste of a long-gone meal had risen in her throat.

It's over in the fraction of an instant, though, replaced by a smile with that same icy calmness.

"Can I help you?"

"Jennifer Lovegood," says Kate with a sneer so natural one would assume she fits right in here.

The receptionist busies herself on the monitors for a moment. "Please sit, Dr Halingrad will be with you shortly."

Kate sits in one of the silvered chairs and again, a careful observer will note the brief expression of distaste at what might be some of the least comfortable sitting furniture in the world.

Everything about this room is designed to remind clients of their own mortality. Ephemeral ferns, finicky orchids, the black colour scheme—and the uncomfortable chairs that remind them subtly of the painful life they endured before Lifetime.

It's about three minutes before a dark-skinned, charcoal-suited doctor, the aforementioned Dr Halingrad, makes his appearance.

Kate stands up at once, possibly anxious to be done with all of this.

There's a polite greeting and the doctor invites "Jennifer" to follow him.

We can skip the walking-down-the-hallways bit—I've gone over and over those recordings and there's nothing valuable there.

You'd think Kate'd have a bit of a peek around, or be scouting the place in some way, or something.

But nope: just stares straight ahead, like she already knows the place—or at the doc as courtesy dictates, while he prattles on and on and on with Lifetime's familiar script: "Change yourself and change the world. Some of our biggest clients have gone on to end hunger in a variety of villages around the world. Think of the good you can do with all this extra time on your hands. Our holistic approach signature treatments state-of-the-art lasting commitment blah blah blah blah blah."

Okay, here's the next interesting part, where he shows her the vault.

The vault has several security cameras, as one would expect for a room housing something so incredibly valuable. I've seen a handful of other vaults before, and they are a similar size to the Walang Kamatayan clinic's waiting room.

This vault feels like a cathedral in comparison. Twenty metres each side if it's an inch, the room glows a soft lapis blue—recessed lighting around the roof and floors designed to manu-

facture mysteried awe in its sup-
plicants.

The walls are hidden by aluminium
cabinets, floor-to-ceiling, all of them,
and the floor is polished concrete, subtly reflecting the light's blue glow. A
series of benches, all aluminium, are
set around the room, about one by two
metres or so. They amplify the blue
lighting, throw it around the room,
reflect it back in gleams and glimmers.

The sterility is possibly useful, but
outside of these clinics, in the transport trucks and so forth, no one stores
the time capsules like this.

The aluminium, the twilight lighting, the drama? It's all for show.

Kate walks in, ushered by the doctor
who's holding open the door for her.
She stops, gives the doctor what he
wants: big round eyes full of wonder,
parted lips, hands twitching at her
sides.

She plays it well, and it seems to satisfy the man, for he chuckles. "Pretty, isn't it."

"It just so… big," Kate gasps.

(And I snicker, every damn time—keep it in your pants, Kate.)

The doctor grins, perfect, even teeth gleaming in the light like a model—or a monster. "Here," he says. "I'll show you."

He turns to the nearest metal cabinet, opens it up. The doors swing on silent hinges—whatever they paid for the cabinets, the craftsman wasn't paid enough.

But that's nothing to what's inside: row upon row upon row of time capsules.

Kate stares, the hunger seeping through just for a moment—but it's okay, it's normal for clients to be hungry for this when they're here.

You can see the moment it dawns on her, though: this cabinet is full of time capsules. And although the doors are closed right now… the cabinet next to it is full of them too.

So's that one, further along.

And the one behind her.

Her eyes go wide. There must be a thousand of them in here; maybe more. "Can I hold one?" she asks, voice a breathless hush.

The doctor smiles indulgingly.

Hands her a capsule.

You have to rewind the recording and watch closely to see her palm the atomiser's tiny tracker onto it.

(Totally aside, I do love that whoever designed them thought to make them capsule-shaped. You know, like a *time - capsule*? A capsule of time, a time capsule… It's a visual pun and I love it.)

(Have you ever held one of those things, but? That weird, tinny, blue taste, the kind of oily residue they leave on your hands like time's just leaking outta them… They give me the creeps, man. Here, hang on, I got one back here somewhere, an empty.)

Item 3: Time Capsule 2.2

A time capsule, about half a foot long and shaped like an old medical capsule, the kind you used to swallow. It's capped with metal at both ends, a gunmetal blue. The length of it is semi-opaque, whitish. If you hold them up to the light, though—sunlight works best, halogen bulbs are okay too, fluoros and incandescent bulbs not so much—the colour changes depending on how full the capsule is. The ones that glow gold are best.

The capsule feels oddly heavy in the hand, like a weighted dumbbell. The sides are sleek and slick and oily, though nothing comes off on your skin, and the capped ends are always cold.

The whole thing smells weird, weird enough to make your skin crawl sometimes if you think on it too long. There's a tinny, metal kind of smell—that's what most people liken it to—but it's more than that, something kind of... blue. Maybe that means it smells like ozone, or oxygen, or pure water. One of those clean, barely-there kind of smells—except with a time capsule, the smell's not barely there. It's strong.

Makes your mouth kind of water, to be honest.

The creepiest thing, though? If you hold one to your ear, you can hear it faintly crackling. Like good dirt, you know? Ever open the lid on a worm farm and listen in the quiet as the worms crackled and rustled their way wetly through the dirt?

I have.

It sounds like that.

And no one has any idea why.

No moving parts, nothing alive in there. Doesn't make sense, but there it is.

Yeah, sure, that one's empty, you can take it. Anyway.
Back to the recording.

The doctor takes the capsule back from Kate, slides it into its rack in the aluminium cabinet, closes the door. He doesn't even lock it; they're so sure of their security, their status.
Doesn't occur to them that other people might want what they have, the ones who can't afford a couple of mill a year.
Doesn't occur to them that some-one might have procured a f—ing

atomiser, when for the same price that someone could essentially achieve immortality with Lifetime's time serum.

Kate follows him from the vault.

He's talking to her about timings and quantities and injection rates, how long the serum takes to work—"You have to allow several weeks for the gene drive to replicate throughout your body enough to notice a difference, sometimes longer. Remember, it takes about seven years for all the cells in your body to be replaced. That's why we recommend seven annual doses initially, and a seven-yearly top-up after that."—and Kate's just nodding along, her heels clicking on the grey linoleum floor of the hallway.

They reach the reception room. Kate shakes the hand offered to her.

"Just chat to Ava here, she'll set you up with an appointment for your first treatment."

Kate nods, the doctor leaves.

Polite smile anchored firmly in place, Kate makes an appointment for a week's time.

She leaves.

We switch briefly to the camera of the street behind the clinic, at the corner of Fourth and Main. Gus in his nondescript silver SUV blends in nicely with the traffic that flows past on the strect, even though he's pulled over on the shoulder of the road.

He doesn't even need to get out of his car.

The laundry truck pulls into the loading dock behind him. You can see him shifting in the car, probably watching the truck through the rearview mirror.

It's a little clumsy in its manoeuvres, knocks over a garbage can and litter from the clinic flies everywhere, white and clear plastic wrappers swooping up into the breeze, spiralling through the traffic on the street.

(I can't help wrinkling my nose at this point, because those wrappers? They're the waste from the special syringes they use to inject the time capsule serum, and to me they always stink of antiseptic. Reminds me of this one time I was ten and had to have a tooth pulled at the dentist.

Nightmare. Urgh.

…Sorry, I know. Back on track.)

The huge, truck-sized roller door of the loading dock clanks open, inch by inch by inch.

There are a couple of shouts. The truck driver hops out, throws open the back doors of the truck.

From the loading dock's internal camera, we watch as he throws a few packing blankets, grey and frayed, out of the way.

A moment later, two people in the clinic's white-with-blue-and-green-trim uniforms wheel out a giant laundry hamper, steel frame with white cotton bag large enough to throw a motorbike in. One of the wheels screams torturously.

The truck driver helps them unclip the bag with the laundry—towels and sheets and dirty uniforms, mostly. He tosses it in the back of the truck.

If you watch very closely, you can see the edge of the bag change shape— see, right there—as outside, still in the front seat of his car, Gus hits the recall button on the atomiser.

The uniform obeys: with the help of its tracer tag, it atomises instantly and is transported into the box of the atomiser.

Back to the outside camera.

Watch carefully.

Gus presses another button on the atomiser—hey, you seen an atomiser before? No? It's… it's like an electrical panel about the size of a paperback novel attached to a chamber about a foot squared.

I hear rumours the military are working on one three times that size. Imagine what you could atomise with that kind of capacity. Scary stuff.

Anyway.

Gus opens the chamber of the atomiser. Pulls out a Lifetime Clinic uniform. Throws it and the atomiser on the passenger's seat, and drives off.

Now we're viewing footage from the camera outside the Lifetime Clinic.

Phil's there, and if we zoom in and enhance the image, it's possible to see the contact lenses in place. If you didn't know he was supposed to have brown eyes, not blue, they'd be impossible to detect.

Not impossible to notice, though; as Gus pulls up to the curb, Kate jumps into the front seat and shimmies into the uniform—and just as the security guard is getting interested in the free show going on in front of him, Phil ducks in front of him, that sardonic smile (See? I told you.) in place.

The guard glances at him, ready to fend him off... And then he notices the lenses.

Look-at-mes, Kate called them earlier, and she's right, because these lenses have been specially designed to capture the attention of any viewer. They enhance Phil's neural pathways, boosting his brainwaves—and putting the guard into an almost soporific stupor, so long as Phil is thinking hard enough about sleep.

(By the by, these are *genius* lil pieces of tech, and I'd give at least a finger to have some. Didn't even know these were in development, and I tell you, I'm pretty good at having my finger to the blackmarket technological pulse. Yeah, even if I do say so myself. Shut up.)

It's an hour after lunch. The road is quiet, pedestrians minimal as the hot sun bakes the asphalt, scenting the world with fuel and melting tar.

Kate gets back into the clinic easily.

Too easily. And not a soul cares.

Phil breaks it off with the guard, and we flick to the internal cameras again. It's the same black-marbled waiting room as before, with its ferns and orchids and tasteful ostentation.

Kate walks in, atomiser in hand disguised as a boxy kind of briefcase, this time in sensible flat shoes that are quiet and muffled on the marble.

Phil follows, and as our receptionist Ava spots Kate and frowns, he intercedes once more. "So," he asks Ava as Kate hustles past. "You got any sandwiches here?"

(And I roll my eyes again, as always.)

We're in the hallway, briefly, watching Kate hustle down the grey path toward the vault.

There's a swipe key in her pocket—we see it as she takes it out a few steps from the vault's door.

One wonders how it got there, how convenient it is that the one, random uniform Gus stole from the laundry hamper just *happened* to have a vault key left behind in it.

Hold onto that thought. We'll return to it.

Kate pauses at the vault door, and it's impossible to know what she's waiting for—until we switch back to the waiting room camera and see Phil in the receptionist's chair, honey-blonde Ava on his lap. She's staring into his contact lenses while he leans around her to type at her keypad.

We can't see the screens, or what he's doing, but it's not hard to guess, because in just another second...

There.

The security footage outside the vault reverts to a loop showing footage from the same time yesterday.

Nothing to see here anymore, thanks to Phil. All is well.

Okay, now we have to switch to the final piece of evidence you guys asked for, the cell phone video recording. Lemme queue it up, just a sec...

Right. Ready?

Last one.

The angle's a bit strange, the person who set it up was obviously trying to be as unobtrusive as possible—we found it propped up on one of clinician's desks in the communal office space opposite the vault. You can see Kate through the doorway, and through that window there, see? The internal window looking out from the office onto the grey hallway?

Whose desk?

Ah, well. Good question. Wait up a min till we're done watching it, then I'll tell you my theory.

Hold onto your metaphorical seatbelt.

Here we go again.

Item 4: Cell Phone Recording - Phone Number 5554-639-2171 163-501B 27/19

Kate's obviously gone in and atomised the capsule, because now she's leaving the vault with the atomiser, gaze darting back and forth like she's still in stealth mode.

It's working for her. Everything's clear. On the recording the only sound we can hear is her footsteps. There doesn't seem to be anyone in the office, no one seems to be bothering her in the hall...

It's all quiet.

She could simply walk out the front

and be done with it all, and they would have won.

Instead, that internal window that separates the office from the hall shatters. Glass flies everywhere, and the view is, let's admit it, spectacular for a moment.

Alarms sound.

If you rewind a moment, you see a ripple in the footage that could indicate a sonic pulse—not strong enough to ruin the footage, but just at the right pitch and frequency to hit that glass and make it go kaboom.

Kate whips around, long hair flying over her face, tangling in her mouth, obscuring her vision.

We hear the front door smash open, hear Gus shout, "Where?"

Phil presumably gives him directions, and we hear heavy footsteps.

Gus is running, but so is everyone else in the clinic—and all of them are running for Kate.

Phil's nowhere to be seen, and footage retrieved from the bakery across the way shows he left the building almost as soon as Gus arrived. (Can't blame him.)

Gus wades in, and it's a battle scene in the hallway: Gus approaching Kate from the front of the building, a swamp of white-clad clinicians and doctors from the rear.

Gus throws a couple of silver golf balls.

They explode into grey and faintly purple mist over the Lifetime staff, who begin sneezing and coughing and wheezing.

They clutch at their chests, throats…

But one of them clutches at Kate.

Holds a scalpel up to her neck.

He's clearly the kind of guy who thinks ahead for situations like this, and he's come to the hallway prepared.

Gus holds his hands up.

Police arrive.

Within moments, Kate and Gus are cuffed and under arrest—but not before Kate can press a button on the atomiser, right before the cuffs go on.

That's the end of the useful footage—the rest just shows clean up and the like.

I mean, you won't have any troubles in court with this one. They clearly did it.

I bet you've still got some questions, though. Like, why would the window smash so suddenly like that, and what caused it? Why was there a camera left lying around to film this all?

And where did the time capsule go, because I know you know they never found it on her, or in the atomiser, or anything.

Well, that one I can answer easy enough.

Took me a couple of hours of re-viewing, but I found it in the end.

See, here? She presses the button on the atomiser, cuffs go on…

And there.

That woman there, the Lifetime one in the top right of the screen? Watch the shape of her pocket before and after.

See? See!

Whatever was in the atomiser goes straight to her, she walks straight out in the kerfuffle, and an hour later, turns in her resignation. Ha! Worked at the clinic for three years and just *bam*, like that, resigned.

What puzzled me, though, is how Kate got the woman tagged. I mean, I went back through the last month or so of footage and I couldn't find a thing.

And why to her? Why not tag the

atomiser's contents back to Gus, or Phil?

Doesn't make sense, right?

Well.

[The squeak of a chair.]

Here's the thing—and yeah, I know I'm getting excited, but you're gonna be too when you hear it.

I think Kate wanted to get caught.

Lemme rewind and show you.

There!

See that look there, where she glances over at the cell phone right as the police cuff her? She knows it's on. She has to, why would she look otherwise?

Which got me thinking, right? Why do something like this, go to all that trouble, only to get caught?

So I did some digging.

I know, a little outside my lane as a transcriber, but you transcribe for long enough you get to know people and you get to know ways of getting things to transcribe, you see what I'm saying?

Here, I think you'll like this.

You know Gus's day job place, Hard!Ware!? Yeah. Turns out their hardware sales are mostly a tax write-off. They make their real money supplying the capsule part of the time capsules. Told you I could smell them when I visited, yeah?

They're Lifetime's biggest supplier, actually. Franchise supplies more than 60% of all Lifetime's capsules.

And here, this one's where it gets *reeeeal* interesting. See this? Gus's birth certificate. Had to pay a guy an arm and a leg to find me that, but it's worth it. Gus is Hard!Ware!'s crown prince, hiding in plain sight: secret son of the big wig owner, but the legally nominated heir.

Go on, react or something! I know the booth's air-con is frigid but you don't have to take that literally, ha!

No? Just gonna stare at it?

Yeah, sure you can take that copy, I got it backed up.

[Patting noise of a hand on a computer terminal.]

Now, about the window, and the cell phone. I reckon they were done by the same person—someone who's been helping Kate for years.

Remember that clinician who ended up with the time capsule?

Well, this is a bit twisty so bear with me, but here.

Check out this document.

Now, look, I dunno half the sciencey words that're going on in here, but the gist of it's easy enough to understand. You know how Lifetime's all like yay lobsters, woo non-degrading telomeres, let's whack some lobster in your DNA and you'll live forever for the low, low price of two million dollars annually for your injection?

Yeah. Well. It ain't just lobsters.

See, best as I can make out, the way

it works is they wrote gene drives to snip out the human telomeres and plug in the lobster ones, right? You inject the serum, it unzips your DNA, snips out the unwanted part—in this case, the human telomeres—and re-places it with something else, the lobster telomeres that don't degrade, don't age.

Ta da! You're practically immortal now, because your cells ain't gonna die anymore.

That's not a stretch, anyone sci-encey could prolly have told me that.

But what's interesting is here…

Hang on, let me scroll down, the document's like five billionty pages long…

Scrolling, scrolling…

I think it's Section J.

Page… 260?

262, yeah, here we go.

So, if I'm reading this right, the

lobster drive isn't the only one they made. You heard of a cuttlefish drive?

Yeah. Neither had I.

Here, look at this.

Unlabelled item: Series of Photographs Showing Decaying Cuttlefish

They literally rot to death. Stinks to high heaven, I've heard, like load of rotten fish sprinkled with dying seaweed. The kind of taste that sticks in your throat and makes you gag, thick as mud.

Yummy. Sounds like my uncle's fridge.

Anyway, look, see this paragraph?

[Tapping sounds.]

Lifetime commissioned a second gene drive, but this one's heritable, so unlike the lobster drive, you don't have to keep going in for boosters—and you pass it on to your kids.

Check out the date on this paper. They started using the cuttlefish drive *ten years before* the time capsules with their lobster DNA came online.

Only it wasn't the rich people getting the cuttlefish drive.

It was everyone else.

[Slamming sound.]

That's why public health's declining at such a rapid rate the last decade. Got nothing to do with the government or health budget or spending or whatever crap. It's Lifetime.

And you know something else? That medicine half the population are hooked on, Astedor? *Lifetime's parent corporation manufactures it.*

And here's the real kicker, the bit I promised you. The lab that published this report on the cuttlefish drive ten years ago?

Aurora Industries, headed by one Ashley Olsen. Kate Olsen's sister.

Here, take a look at her.

Unlabelled item: Photograph of a blonde woman staring confidently at the camera with light, 'natural' make-up, wearing a white lab coat. The resemblance to Kate is unquestionable.

Look familiar? I mean other than to Kate. No?

Here. Check this out. I'll rewind the footage again, give you a look at that clinician the life capsule went to.

See?

It's Ashley. Freaking. Olsen.

[A seat creaks.]

Three years! Three years she worked at the Walang Kamatayan Lifetime Clinic, and no one suspected a thing!

They did it together, they must have. The laundry, the swipe card—the window and the cell phone.

Which begs the final question: Why the cell phone? Why record it?

And here's my final gambit. They knew the chances of getting a capsule out of there were minuscule. Even the atomiser only helped them at the time, because you can bet your ass Lifetime would have put every dollar they had behind a legal team to track down the culprit.

So why do it?

I'll tell you why.

Here, I'll lower the screen. Lean in, this deserves to be dramatic.

They did it like this, because they *wanted* the transcription tech to go digging.

That's me, to clarify.

[Chair creak.]

Lifetime's busted, mate. A gene drive that gets passed onto your kids and makes your cells decay faster, weakens your immune system? That Malaise crap they bin talking about on the news all year ain't no fake news. Lifetime invented it. *Ten years ago.*

This gets out, there'll be the court case of the century, and ain't nobody alive can stop it.

...What do you mean, that's enough?

No, no one else knows yet, I only finished wading through that long-ass paper this morning on my break.

No, you may *not* have my computer terminal, thanks.

Look, just sit here and shut up for a second like you've been so good at doing so far, and I'm gonna go get my boss.

[A rattle.]

...Why is the door locked?

*** * END RECORDING, SOUND BOOTH 108 061248 154801 * ***

Ashley Olsen nodded as the recording ended and the unnamed informant who'd brought her the tape shot her a questioning glance. "Yep," she said. "That plus the match between the gene drive in the time serum and the cuttlefish drive that my lab found is enough to break them. Thanks. I appreciate it. Here."

She handed over a time capsule.

Her informant held it up to the sunlight streaming in through the window just to make sure.

Smiled, when he saw it was bright gold.

"Good luck, then," he said. "I hope it turns out the way you want."

Ashley snorted. "I'll bet you do."

BREAKING NEWS
Lifetime Clinic implicated in Malaise scandal

Geneticist Ashley Olsen working for independent lab Aurora Industries has confirmed to the press that the proprietary gene drive component in Lifetime Clinic's famous time capsules matches the drive recently uncovered as the cause of the colloquially-named Malaise, a pandemic previously thought to be a hoax affecting sizeable portions of AC's population over the last five years.

The news that a gene drive was behind the Malaise has sparked public outrage, with calls for bans on gene drives altogether. But with so many politicians heavily invested in Lifetime Clinic's proprietary product, stricter legislation surrounding the use of gene drives may prove elusive.

In the meantime, Aurora Industries have assembled a legal team to determine whether Lifetime Clinic and its parent corporation General Investments Co. can be held liable for the detrimental effects of their non-consensual release into the public of what has been nicknamed the 'cuttlefish drive'.

THE MAKING OF *CAUGHT IN THE ACT*

For the longest of times, I had in my head that I needed to write a story about someone stealing time, as in physically, time itself. I think *Doctor Who* is to blame: Season 8, Episode 5, *Time Heist*.

Come on. Time Heist? And then the story was *not* about stealing time?

It was a good episode still, but given the name, totally a wasted opportunity right there.

So. I needed to write a story about stealing time.

Caught In The Act? Not at all the story that I thought I was going to write about stealing time.

This one was for a course I completed in January 2020, and I had literally 24 hours to write the story. I remembered that, but I'd completely forgotten until I went back and reread this story in preparation for it becoming an Inklet that there had been another part of the assignment: the story had to be in response to an article I'd read in *The Best American Science and Nature Writing of 2019*, edited by Sy Montgomery.

I thought I'd write in response to the article about the vapours in the locations of the Ancient Greek oracles, or the decline of the insect population.

I didn't expect to choose "Deleting A Species", an article by Rowan Jacobsen about scientists working to engineer a heritable gene drive that will make a species of mosquito infertile.

But I sat down, wrote the first line… and this strange, odd little thing of a story unspooled from there.

I kept having to go back and refine the opening, the first half, the middle, all the bits that had come before in order to have it make sense, and it wasn't until I was at least halfway through that I realised that *this* was not only a story about gene drives, it was also the story about stealing time.

I'd expected something a bit more… linear.

A bit more… obvious.

The girl out to steal more time for her sister. Something urban fantasy-eque, perhaps. Dystopian. Maybe even young adult.

I did not expect… this.

But really, I was writing about stealing time. Why on earth did I assume that that would result in a straightforward story??

Read more by Amy Laurens!

RUSH JOB

ON THE POLISHED-WHITE PERSPEX DESK BY THE holovid, the tiny grey printer chattered. The little stream of paper it was sending out into the dim room was no more than a handsbreadth across, and in the blue light of the sleeping screens the paper glowed cerulean.

Jamie Evans leaned back in her moulded desk chair, waiting for the printer to finish. The warm scent of the ink clouded around her and she drummed her fingers on the desk, impatient to see what the orders would bring.

The printer chattered on.

Jamie glanced up at the holoscreens that towered from her desk surface right up to the roof, wrapping around her in a glowing blue semi-circle in the small, dark control room of her shuttle. The screens continued their sleep though, devoid of any new information.

Out of habit, she checked the nav-system: all clear, everything still on track, the shuttle scheduled to arrive at the space station Aphelion in a little over two hours.

Jamie drummed her fingers again as the printer continued its chatter.

Damn thing never was fast enough.

She stretched languidly in her chair, briefly considered that she should maybe grab something to eat as her stomach rumbled, then decided not as memories of her last visit to Aphelion surfaced.

Aphelion's marketplace was famous throughout the entirety of clean space, with every kind of food—and every kind of human—in attendance. Along with a fair few other things, including everything you usually had to travel to Clan Space for.

Jamie's lips quirked. Last time, she'd come away with a lifelong love for pecan cheesecake, a pocket scanner that should have taken two months and four thousand bucks to source if she'd done it legal, and a voucher for a dinner at Maxador, rumoured to be the best restaurant in not just this quadrant, but the entire galaxy.

Even the Witch Clans, it was rumoured, couldn't do better than Maxador.

Jamie stretched again and sighed. It was fifty-fifty whether she'd have time to cash in on that dinner on this trip. It all hinged on that strip of paper now trailing over the edge of the desk from the little printer.

The printer beeped, green light flashing.

Ha. At last. You'd have thought, Jamie mused, that in this day and age someone could invent a cryptron printer that was faster.

Jamie leaned forward, tore off the strip of paper, and turned it over. Arcane-looking symbols covered it in neat, diagonal lines. She squinted. She'd been receiving her orders in cryptron for eight years now, and despite the fact that it was designed to be an infallibly uncrackable cipher unless you had one of the patented and heavily legislated readers, some days she felt she was getting the hang of it. That series of markings there, for example.

Her heart sped up.

Unless she was highly mistaken, that little cluster meant a job with a tight deadline.

Jamie spun the chair around, tapped the control panel on the other side of desk to wake the reader, and fed the long slip of paper into the slot in the interface.

A portion of the screen at the lower

left lit up, white code streaming past on a blue background, designed not to provide any actually information, but merely to make it look like the machine was doing something useful. Jamie knew. She'd copied all the code down in her first year and broken it. *Lorem ipsum dolor sit amet...* It was all nonsense.

She drummed her fingers again.

The scent of warm spices curled around her.

"Hello-Alex?"

"Hello, Jamie," the ship's AI responded in soothing, neutral tones.

"Why can I smell yellow curry?"

"It is thirteen hundred ship time. It is time for you to ingest sustenance."

Jamie sighed. Forgetting to reschedule the automatic meal system wasn't the worst thing in the world. And if this really was a rush job the cryptron reader was presently decoding, maybe it was better to eat here first.

The lower-left screen flashed green. The torrent of nonsense code gave way to a series of runic markings on screen—Cyrillic, a millennia-dead language revived explicitly for this purpose when cryptron was invented, because there was no point having an unhackable cipher if you also had a machine that could simply translate it into Standard. There were legislations around ownership of the readers, sure, but it would be stupid to assume that in the whole history and use of cryptron, no one would ever illegally procure a reader. Or crack the code.

Cyrillic, though, Jamie could read no problem. The gist of the situation was this: in about nine hours, a deal was going down somewhere in the marketplace on Aphelion, probably Sector Q. Maybe P.

A rare—and priceless—stolen item was being traded.

The government needed the item

back. Jamie was to retrieve it.

There were more details, of course: general description of the item, possible parties involved in the trade, blah blah, etc etc.

Jamie stopped. Squinted at the page. Reread it, just to make sure her Cyrillic wasn't off.

The item she was supposed to collect was a spherical, gelatinous object about two feet in diameter. It was listed as organic, virtually indestructible, and preferring vacuum for long-term transport.

Jamie squinted again. "Hello-Alex?"

"Hello, Jamie."

"Read this." She motioned at one of Alex's many camera eyes set around the room, their lenses no more than an inch across. "What does this sound like to you?"

"Item category best fits that of a space egg."

Jamie's stomach flipped. "Yeah. That's what I thought."

There were still a few surviving species that did space eggs of that size, shape and colour. It was plausible—and probable—that this was no particularly big deal, just a species the IGP wanted their hands on. This was not the 2600s. Surrofish had died out over 400 years ago.

It was not a surrofish egg, because that would be stupid—and disastrous.

Jamie chewed at the inside of her lip.

A century or two after humans colonised space, they'd realised they weren't alone. There were other creatures out there in the black, not sentient, but smart in their own ways. These creatures lived in the vacuum, a complex, delicate ecosystem built on living particles similar to tardigrades—single-celled and nearly indestructible.

They formed the bottom of a food

web as complex and varied as the one built on plankton. And for the most part, these creatures of vacuum were about as dangerous to humans as ocean creatures were—keep out of their way and they'd keep out of yours.

Then the Witches, a group of super-powered and highly xenophobic humans, had found the surrofish, whose eggs could support the bacteria the Witches used to maintain their super-powers—and which sent normal humans fatally insane.

A surrofish egg could survive vacuum indefinitely, and at only two-feet in width, they were nigh undetectable to radars attuned to larger threats.

And loaded up with Witch bacteria, they could seed the terraforming of an entire planet, letting loose a pathogen that would destroy any clean humans on the planet within months.

It was the galactic equivalent to all-out nuclear warfare, and it only ended when the IGP—Inter-Galactic Police, the enforcement arm of the united government of clean-human space—had engineered a gene drive that sent the surrofish extinct.

A tiny, possibly concerned beep. "Is anything wrong?" Alex enquired.

Jamie shook her head, hauling herself out of the dark well of her thoughts. "No. I'm being absurd. Alarmist. Like the plague, you know? Mention a rat infestation and people's minds *still* go back to the great Earth plagues of the 1400s."

"I am aware of this connection."

Jamie sighed. So she had to retrieve a space egg. There were plenty of species that laid space eggs. Totally no big deal.

And if she worked fast enough, her IGP orders wouldn't interfere with her plans to see Nathaniel.

Again.

She rechecked the navsys. One hour

and forty-six minutes to prep. Plenty of time.

Right after she ate that curry.

Keep reading! Head to www.inkprintpress.com/amylaurens/witchblue/rushjob/ to buy your copy now!

ABOUT THE AUTHOR

AMY LAURENS is an Australian author of fantasy fiction for all ages. Some days, the number of stories she still wants to write makes immortality on this planet almost seem worthwhile...

Amy has won an Aurealis for her fantasy novella, *Bones Of The Sea*. She also written the award-winning portal-fantasy *Sanctuary* series about Edge, a 13-year-old girl forced to move to a small country town because of witness protection, the humorous fantasy *Kaditeos* series, following newly graduated Evil Overlord Mercury as she attempts to acquire a castle, the young adult series *Storm Foxes* about love and magic and family in small town Australia, and a whole host of short stories and non-fiction.

INKLETS

Collect them all! Released on the 1st and 15th
of each month.

Dancer, Dreamer
Seer
LIANA BROOKS

As Time
Whirls Slowly
Past
AMY LAURENS

Far More
Satisfying
Than Hell
AMY LAURENS

Just
Another Day
In Hell
LIANA BROOKS

Moon AND
Morning
AMY LAURENS

Some
Impropriety
Expected
AMY LAURENS

NEON SNOW
LIANA BROOKS

Reincarnation
LIANA BROOKS

More Than
Mushrooms
AMY LAURENS

DOUBLE ISSUE
INKLET #092
How To Make A Star
& The World Ended
LIANA BROOKS

INKLET #093
CAUGHT
IN THE ACT
AMY LAURENS

INKLET #094
ANUBIS
Has Sent You
Six Souls
LIANA BROOKS

INKLET #095
PRAYER TO A
GODDESS
LIANA BROOKS

INKLET #096
Love In The
Time Of Corona
AMY LAURENS

INKLET #097
RECRUITMENT
AMY LAURENS

INKLET #098
IDENTITY
Theft 101
LIANA BROOKS

INKLET #099
Curses
With Benefits
AMY LAURENS

INKLET #100
NECROMANCER
TROUBLES
LIANA BROOKS